Postman Pat®'s Magic Christmas

SIMON AND SCHUSTER

SIMON AND SCHUSTER
First published in 2003 in Great Britain by Pocket Books
an imprint of Simon & Schuster UK Ltd
Africa House, 64-78 Kingsway, London WC2B 6AN

This edition published in 2006 by Simon & Schuster UK Ltd
A CBS COMPANY

A CIP catalogue record for this book is available from the British Library upon request

ISBN 1-416-92633-X
EAN 9781416926337

Printed in China

10 9 8 7 6 5 4 3 2 1

It was Christmas Eve morning in Greendale and Pat was getting ready for work.
"I'm going to dress up like Santa Claus at the Christmas party tonight," he told Jess. "It's a surprise. I can't wait to see everyone's faces when I – I mean – Santa walks in."

Sara was in the kitchen baking a cake for Santa.
"Mum," said Julian, "I can't think what to ask Santa
to bring me and it's Christmas Eve!"
"I'm sure you'll think of something," comforted Sara.
No one noticed that cheeky Jess was about to steal a
bag of flour.

Pat was almost ready to leave. "Bye everyone," he called. "I've got a busy day today delivering parcels and cards. Thank goodness it's not snowing!"

"Snow!!" beamed Julian hurrying to finish his letter. "Dear Santa, what I want for Christmas is… snow!" Pat promised to post the letter before he started work.

Just then, Julian's friend, Charlie Pringle, arrived. Charlie was really excited about the Christmas party. "There's a secret special guest, too," he told Pat and Julian.

"Cool," breathed Julian. "Do you know who it is, Dad?"
"Hmmm… maybe…" Pat chuckled.

"I wish it would snow," said Julian, looking out of the window. Charlie noticed Jess's floury footprints leading from a bag of flour.
"I know how to make it snow," he laughed.

"Oh no!" said Pat, standing at the front door. "Look. It's snowing!"
The two boys had emptied the flour out of the bedroom window. It looked just like snow, sprinkling to the ground!

At the post office Mrs Goggins gave Pat a huge pile of parcels and
Christmas cards.

Pat was right. It *was* going to be a busy day! His first delivery was to the
train station. Pat handed Ajay a huge box.

"Oh good, I've been waiting for this," said Ajay, taking a large Christmas
wreath out of the box. He carefully placed it on the front of the
Greendale Rocket. "Ahhh, perfect," he sighed. "I wouldn't want her to
miss out on the festivities."

Julian, Charlie and Bill were trying to sledge outdoors. But it was no good. The sledge just wouldn't budge without snow.
"I asked Santa to bring snow," sighed Julian. "Maybe Dad hasn't delivered my letter yet."

Bill suggested fixing some old skateboard wheels underneath the sledge.
It worked perfectly! Soon all the children were taking turns whizzing
down the hill on the new, super-fast Wheelie Sledge.
"This is brilliant!" hooted Julian.

Driving along on his rounds Pat noticed a stranger standing on the side of the road. He had a big white beard, big black boots and a red hat with a white pom-pom on the end. He looked *very* familiar.

"Hello, are you lost?" asked Pat.
"Er, yes, I think I am," answered the stranger
in a jolly sort of voice. "I'm trying to get to
Greendale. I only get out here once a year and
my vehicle runs much better in the snow."
A sudden gust of wind sent the stranger's hat flying into a
field. Pat offered to give him a lift if the stranger didn't mind
coming with Pat on his rounds. "Oh no," said the stranger, with a
twinkle in his eye. "It'll be nice to see how it's usually done!"
Pat stared at the stranger. He really was *very* familiar.

Everyone in Greendale was busy preparing for Christmas. Pat and the stranger were delivering the letters. They had parcels for everyone in Greendale. Pat was worried that they wouldn't be finished in time for the party.

He was so busy he didn't notice that something magical was happening.

While Pat wasn't looking, the stranger
clicked his fingers – **CLICK** – and the letters flew through the air and into the
correct letterboxes! **CLICK!**
CLICK! And the same with the parcels!
CLICK! Soon, everything was delivered.

"I wish it would snow," moaned Julian. "I want to make a snowman. I wonder if Santa even got my letter?"
"We don't need snow to build a snowman," said Katy Pottage. The children built a scarecrow snowman instead.

Julian found the stranger's red-and-white hat and put it on the scarecrow's head.

"There you go," said Julian. "He's the best no-snowman ever!"
Soon it was time to go home.

Pat and the stranger were on their way home too when, suddenly, "Ooo-errrr, help!" cried Pat. The van slipped and slithered on a muddy patch of a road, sending them into a field. Pat got out to look and stepped straight into a muddy puddle.

"Here, you can borrow these," said the stranger, handing Pat a pair of big black boots. "I usually carry a spare pair." Together they dug the van out of the mud and were soon on their way again.

In the middle of a lane the stranger suddenly asked Pat to stop the van. "Are you sure?" protested Pat. "Quite sure, thanks," the stranger assured him, getting out of the van.

Pat got out to say goodbye but the stranger had disappeared. Pat was very surprised. "Oh, where did he go?" He didn't hear the sound of jingling bells as the red-and-white hat disappeared from the no-snowman's head.

It was getting dark and Pat still had letters to deliver. All of Greendale was decorated with Christmas lights. It looked beautiful.
"I'm going to be late for the party," worried Pat. "I won't have time to change."

"Merry Christmas Santa," said Sara, putting a piece of cake and a glass of juice beside the fireplace. "Come on, Julian!" she called. "Let's go to the party."

At the Christmas party the whole village was having fun, dancing and chatting and playing games.
Suddenly, the door burst open and in walked...

"Santa!" cried all the children. "It's Santa." It *was* Santa and he had presents for everyone. The children clustered around him but all too soon, Santa had to say goodbye.

"Merry Christmas everyone!" he laughed. Then he waved goodbye one last time and disappeared.

A moment later a breathless Pat rushed in! Julian rushed to tell him all about Santa. "What?" panted Pat. "But I've only just got here."

Everyone thought that Pat had pretended to be Santa.
"Nice one Pat," laughed Ajay, noticing Pat's big black boots.
"Och yes, Pat!" chortled Mrs Goggins. "You made a fine Father Christmas."
Pat was confused. So was Julian.

"If Dad was pretending to be Santa, where's the real Santa?" he asked. "Santa's so busy on Christmas Eve that he has helpers like Daddy," Sara explained. Julian was sad. He thought the *real* Santa had come to the party.

That night, as he lay in bed, Julian heard a strange jingling sound from downstairs. He went to investigate. And who was there, putting presents under the tree? Santa!

"Santa, it's really you," cried Julian.

Pat and Sara joined Julian in the doorway.

"Ho, ho, hello Julian. I hope you like the boots, Pat," said Santa, "and Sara, this cake is delicious."

Before they could answer Santa had disappeared with a jingling of bells.

"Ho ho. And I've left an extra present for you outside," twinkled Santa's voice.

They rushed to the front door.
"Snow!" cried Julian. "It's snowing."
And it was! Beautiful, thick, white snow covered Greendale.
"Thank you, Santa!" called Julian.
A bright light whizzed across the sky like a shooting star.
"Ho, ho, ho! Merry Christmas everyone," laughed Santa.